I PROMISE
I'LL FIND YOU

I PROMISE
I'LL FIND YOU

WRITTEN BY HEATHER PATRICIA WARD
ILLUSTRATED BY SHEILA McGRAW

FIREFLY BOOKS

A FIREFLY BOOK

Design: Sheila McGraw
Typesetting: Parker Typesetting

Cataloguing in Publication Data

Ward, Heather P., 1967-
  I promise I'll find you

ISBN 1-55209-094-9

I. McGraw, Sheila, 1949-   . II. Title.

PS8595.A73I2 1994   jC8II'.54   C94-931924-4
PZ8.3.W37Ip 1994

Published in Canada by:
Firefly Books Ltd.
3680 Victoria Park Avenue
Willowdale, Ontario, Canada
M2H 3K1

Published in the United States by:
Firefly Books (U.S.) Inc.
P.O. Box 1325
Ellicott Station
Buffalo, NY 14205

Printed and bound in Canada

This book is dedicated with love
to all of the missing children in the world
and to the memory of Kelly Cook.

If I had a little rowboat,

I'd row across the sea.

I'd row, row, row,

And I'd bring you back to me.

If I had a little airplane,

I'd fly across the sky.

I'd look and look and look for you,

As every day went by.

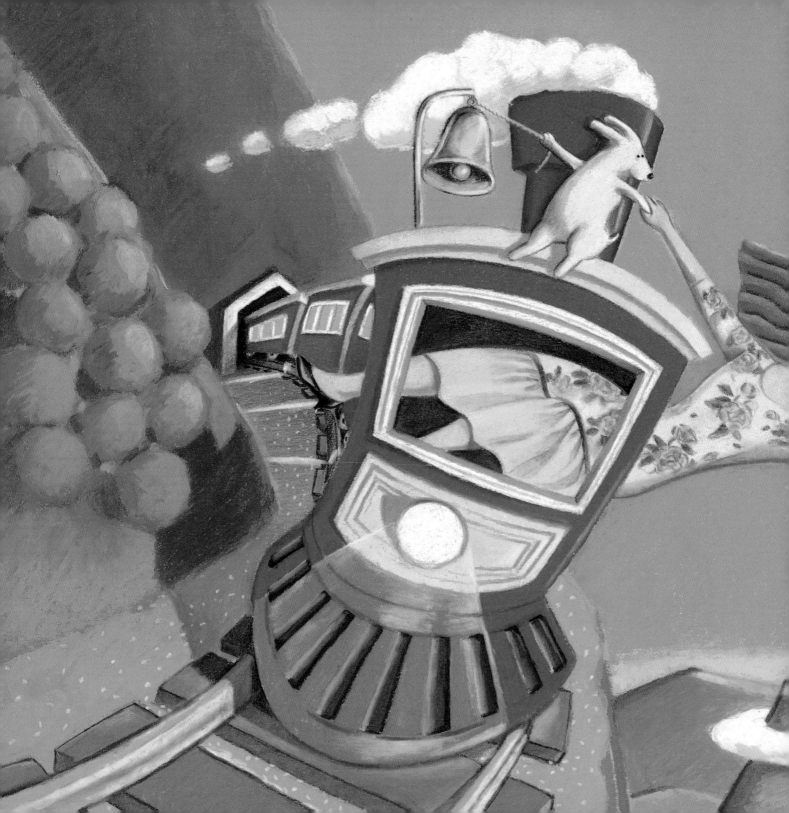

If I had a little choo-choo train,

I'd chug on down the track.

I'd chug until I found you,

And then I'd bring you back.

If I had a little horsie,

I'd make that horsie run.

He'd run and run and look for you,

Until the day was done.

If I had a little racecar,

I'd race the whole world twice.

I'd find you and I'd keep you,

Oh, that would be so nice.

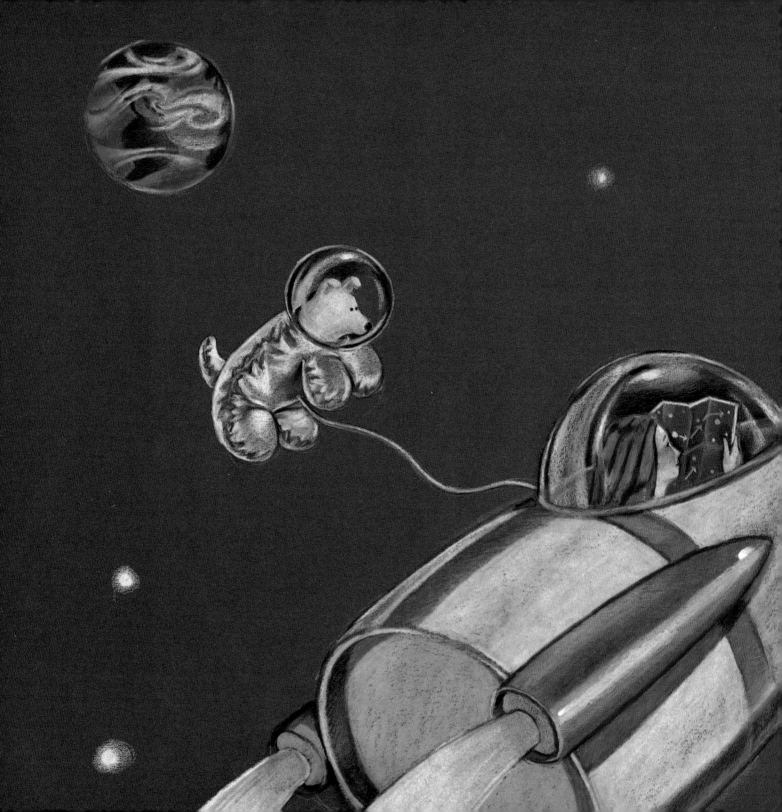

If I had a little rocket ship,

I'd shoot up to the moon.

Oh, that would be the fastest way,

I'd have you really soon.

If I had a little submarine,

I'd go beneath the sea.

I'd scout around to find you,

And hold you next to me.

If I had a little green balloon,

I'd fly all through the air.

I'd pick you up and bring you home,

And you would know I care.

If I had a little motorbike,

I'd ride across the land.

I'd find you and I'd reach for you,

And you would take my hand.

And if I had no other way,

I'd walk or crawl or run.

I'd search to the very ends of the earth,

For you my precious one.

So remember this my darling,

For it is very true.

If ever you're apart from me,

I'll search till I find you.

Heather Patricia Ward lives in Hanna, Alberta. She is the mother of four children. This is her first book.

Sheila McGraw lives in Toronto, and is the mother of two sons. She is the illustrator of the best-selling book *Love You Forever*, and the author of *Papier Mâché Today*, *Papier Mâché For Kids*, *Gifts Kids Can Make*, *Dolls Kids Can Make*, and *Soft Toys To Sew*.

A portion of the author's proceeds from the sale of this book will benefit child-locating agencies.